MEDUSA'S STONY STARE

A RETELLING BY
JESSICA GUNDERSON

ILLUSTRATED BY
RICH PELLEGRINO

Raintree

CAST OF CHARACTERS

ACRISIOS: king of Argos, and father of Danae

DANAE: daughter of Acrisios, and mother of Perseus

ZEUS: immortal king of all gods

PERSEUS: son of Danae and Zeus, and grandson of Acrisios

DICTYS: fisherman who loves Danae

POLYDECTES: king of the island of Seriphos

MEDUSA: mortal daughter of Phorcys and Ceto

ATHENA: goddess of war

POSEIDON: god of the sea

HIPPODAMEIA: a woman who King Polydectes claims he wants to marry

HERMES: messenger of the gods

STYGIAN NYMPHS: nature goddesses

GRAEAE SISTERS: sisters who were born as old women

WORDS TO KNOW

ARGOS ancient Greek city

MOUNT OLYMPUS home of the Olympian gods

MYTH story from ancient times

SERIPHOS Greek island in the Aegean Sea

VALLEY OF THE GORGONS Medusa's home

VANITY too much regard for one's own accomplishments or appearance

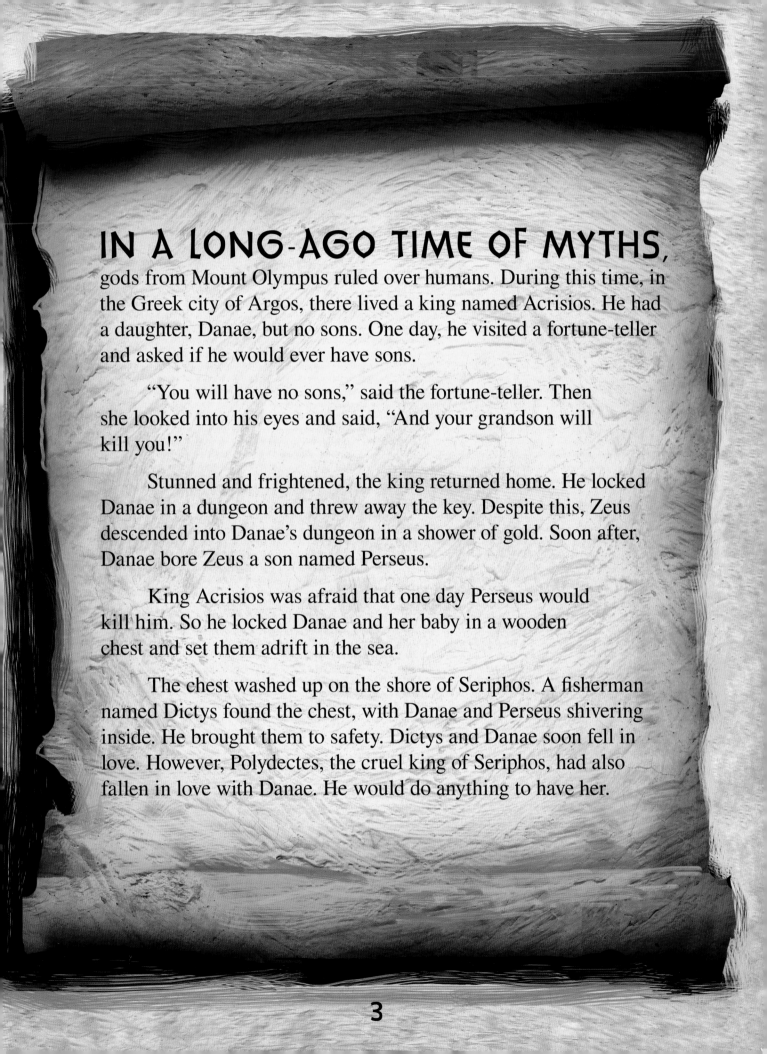

IN A LONG-AGO TIME OF MYTHS,

gods from Mount Olympus ruled over humans. During this time, in the Greek city of Argos, there lived a king named Acrisios. He had a daughter, Danae, but no sons. One day, he visited a fortune-teller and asked if he would ever have sons.

"You will have no sons," said the fortune-teller. Then she looked into his eyes and said, "And your grandson will kill you!"

Stunned and frightened, the king returned home. He locked Danae in a dungeon and threw away the key. Despite this, Zeus descended into Danae's dungeon in a shower of gold. Soon after, Danae bore Zeus a son named Perseus.

King Acrisios was afraid that one day Perseus would kill him. So he locked Danae and her baby in a wooden chest and set them adrift in the sea.

The chest washed up on the shore of Seriphos. A fisherman named Dictys found the chest, with Danae and Perseus shivering inside. He brought them to safety. Dictys and Danae soon fell in love. However, Polydectes, the cruel king of Seriphos, had also fallen in love with Danae. He would do anything to have her.

In the Valley of the Gorgons, far from the island of Seriphos, lived a child named Medusa. As Medusa grew up, she realized she was different to her two sisters. Her sisters were not pleasant to look upon, but Medusa was beautiful. Her golden hair shone upon her head. Her eyes and smile were bewitching. Anyone who looked at her was entranced.

Something else was different about Medusa. Her sisters were immortal, which meant they would never die. However, Medusa was mortal. One day, she would die.

Medusa did not think about her mortality. Instead, she spent her days looking in the mirror, pleased with her beauty.

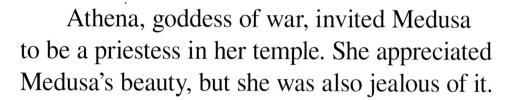

Athena, goddess of war, invited Medusa to be a priestess in her temple. She appreciated Medusa's beauty, but she was also jealous of it.

Athena often caught Medusa staring at her own reflection. "My temple is no place for vanity," Athena warned. "This is a sacred place."

Medusa nodded, but after Athena left, she turned back to the mirror. Athena's words did not matter. Medusa cared only about her own beauty.

One day, Poseidon, god of the sea, came to Athena's temple. When he saw Medusa, he was amazed by her loveliness. He approached her and grabbed her arm. "Who are you?" he demanded. "Have you a husband?"

"No, I am unmarried," replied Medusa, a little frightened but also pleased that Poseidon had noticed her.

"Then I shall have you, girl!" Poseidon thundered triumphantly.

Medusa tried to break free of his grasp, but the god was too strong. She could not get away.

At that moment, Athena returned to her temple and saw Poseidon embracing Medusa. She was enraged, but she hid behind her shield until Poseidon was gone. Then she revealed herself to Medusa and cried, "You have tempted Poseidon in my sacred temple!"

Trembling, Medusa begged Athena to let her go unpunished. However, Athena had the perfect punishment in mind.

"Your beauty will never tempt another," Athena snarled. "Your beauty is no more!"

With that horrible curse, Athena turned Medusa's golden ringlets into coils of writhing snakes. She turned her skin into scales and her hands into claws. Beautiful Medusa had become a hideous monster.

Medusa ran from Athena's temple in horror. A man passing by stopped to stare at her. His lips curled in disgust, and then his face froze. He had turned into stone.

Medusa was startled, but her horror quickly changed to delight. "My ugliness is more powerful than my beauty could ever have been," she thought, petting the snakes that hissed in her ears. She laughed wickedly as she walked back to the Valley of the Gorgons.

Soon, the story of Medusa had spread across the land. On the island of Seriphos, King Polydectes listened to the tale with interest. Just as Athena had wished for Medusa's beauty, Polydectes also wanted what he could not have: Danae, mother of Perseus.

Polydectes knew that Danae was in love with Dictys, and that Perseus would stop any other man from marrying his mother. He also knew that Perseus knew of his feelings towards Danae. So, Polydectes wanted to get rid of Perseus. When he heard the horrible tale of the monster Medusa, he had a brilliant idea.

Polydectes called his people to his palace. He announced that he would like to take Hippodameia as his bride. "Each family must bring me an engagement gift," he commanded, knowing that Perseus would not be able to afford a gift.

One by one, the families of Seriphos came forward to offer their gifts to Polydectes.

Perseus approached the king empty-handed. "I have no gold to buy a gift," he said. "But I will do anything you want, as long as you stay away from my mother."

Polydectes smiled. His plan was working. "Anything I want, you say? Well, in that case, I want you to bring me the head of Medusa!"

"The Gorgon who turns men into stone?" Perseus asked, trembling.

"The very one," the king said, still smiling. "If you bring me the monster's head, I will marry Hippodameia. If you don't succeed, I will marry your mother instead."

Perseus had no choice. "I will meet your challenge," he agreed.

The king laughed as Perseus walked away. "How will Perseus slay Medusa without looking at her?" he thought. "The boy is as good as dead, and Danae will be mine!"

That night Perseus walked along the seashore, wondering how he would succeed in the challenge. Then he saw two figures, a man and a woman, rise from the water. The woman carried a shield that glinted in the moonlight.

"I am the goddess Athena," she said. "And this is Hermes, messenger of the gods."

Perseus bowed humbly.

"I know Medusa well," Athena went on, "for it was I who turned her into a monster. I can help you to slay her."

"How?" asked Perseus.

Athena handed Perseus her shield. "You cannot look directly at Medusa," she warned. "Instead, look at her reflection in this shield, and you will not turn into stone."

Hermes also had a gift for Perseus. He held out his sickle. "This sickle will be your weapon. With only one blow, it will lop off the monster's head," he said.

Athena told Perseus that he would also need the help of the Stygian nymphs. "Only the Graeae sisters know where the nymphs live. You will have to convince the Graeae to tell you."

Athena guided Perseus to the three Graeae sisters, who were half-swan and had long necks. They had only a single eye and tooth that they shared between them.

The Graeae were not friendly. They tossed the eye and tooth from one to the other, mocking Perseus. "We shall never tell you where the nymphs live!" they hissed.

Perseus jumped between them and caught the eye in one hand and the tooth in the other. "Now you shall tell me," he declared. "For if you don't, I will not return your precious eye and tooth."

Defeated, the Graeae sisters sighed. "You will find the nymphs in the woods beyond the mountain," one told him.

Perseus travelled to the Stygian nymphs, who were much more helpful than the Graeae sisters. They gave him gifts to help slay Medusa.

"Here is a bag to carry Medusa's head," one nymph said.

"These winged sandals will help you fly away after you have slain the monster," said another.

"Here is a magic helmet that will make you invisible," a third nymph offered.

Perseus thanked them and took the gifts. Then he started for the Valley of the Gorgons, where he would face the feared monster Medusa.

Meanwhile, Medusa was enjoying her new power. All around her the valley was filled with the stone bodies of those who had tried to defeat her. She revelled in the terror that was frozen on each of their faces.

"I should thank Athena," Medusa chuckled to her sisters. "She thought she was cursing me, but she made me invincible. I, a mere mortal, have a godlike power," she roared.

Suddenly the snakes surrounding Medusa's head sent up a loud hiss. She knew someone was approaching, but she felt no fear. "He who dares to approach me will soon be dead!" she declared.

Perseus descended the hill into the valley, holding up his shield. Medusa's reflection appeared in it, her hair of snakes waving and hissing. Perseus charged forward, the sickle in his hand.

Suddenly, the gleam of the sickle caught Medusa's eye. She turned to see Perseus holding it up above her, and she let out a sickening scream. But it was too late.

With one strong blow, Perseus sliced Medusa's neck. Her head rolled to the ground, and her serpents gave one final hiss and died.

Furious, Medusa's sisters rushed at him.

Perseus put on the helmet of invisibility and the winged sandals. As he escaped into the sky, he could see the confused sisters far below him.

Perseus flew for a long time. When he finally returned to Seriphos, he went straight to King Polydectes' palace.

Polydectes was surprised to see Perseus. "You have failed!" he said. "No man could return alive –"

He never finished his sentence.

Perseus closed his eyes and took Medusa's head from the bag. The evil king froze into stone!

Perseus' mother, Danae, was now free to marry the man she had always loved.

That night Athena appeared to Perseus along the seashore. "Did you succeed?" she asked him.

"Yes. Thank you for your help," he said as he held out the bag with Medusa's head. "I'd like you to have this."

Athena smiled. "It will be a most valuable weapon," she said. She attached the head to her shield and disappeared into the sea.

www.raintreepublishers.co.uk
Visit our website to find out
more information about
Raintree books.

To order:
☎ Phone 0845 6044371
▤ Fax +44 (0) 1865 312263
▥ Email myorders@raintreepublishers.co.uk

Customers from outside the UK please telephone +44 1865 312262

Raintree is an imprint of Capstone Global Library Limited, a company incorporated
in England and Wales having its registered office at 7 Pilgrim Street, London, EC4V 6LB
– Registered company number: 6695582

Text © Picture Window Books 2012
First published in the United Kingdom in 2012
The moral rights of the proprietor have been asserted.

We would like to thank Terry Flaherty, Professor of English at
Minnesota State University for his advice and expertise.

Editors: Shelly Lyons and Vaarunika Dharmapala
Designer: Alison Thiele
Art Director: Nathan Gassman
Production Specialist: Sarah Bennett
The illustrations in this book were created with watercolours, gouache, acrylics, and digital technology.

ISBN 978 1 406 24302 4 (paperback)
16 15 14 13 12
10 9 8 7 6 5 4 3 2 1

British Library Cataloguing in Publication Data
A full catalogue record for this book is available from the British Library.